For our son Sky

ROBOT & AVOCADO

By:
Lucas
Elrod

On a Bright and sunny day,
Allen the avocado was
flying his kite at the park.

Some clouds started to block the sun, and the wind started to blow!

Allens kite flew into the
tree and got stuck.

Allen was sad...

Allen could not get his kite down.

Rob the robot saw the little avocado by the tree crying.

"Hello my name is Rob, did you need some help?" Asked Rob

"Yes please, my kite got stuck in the tree" said Allen

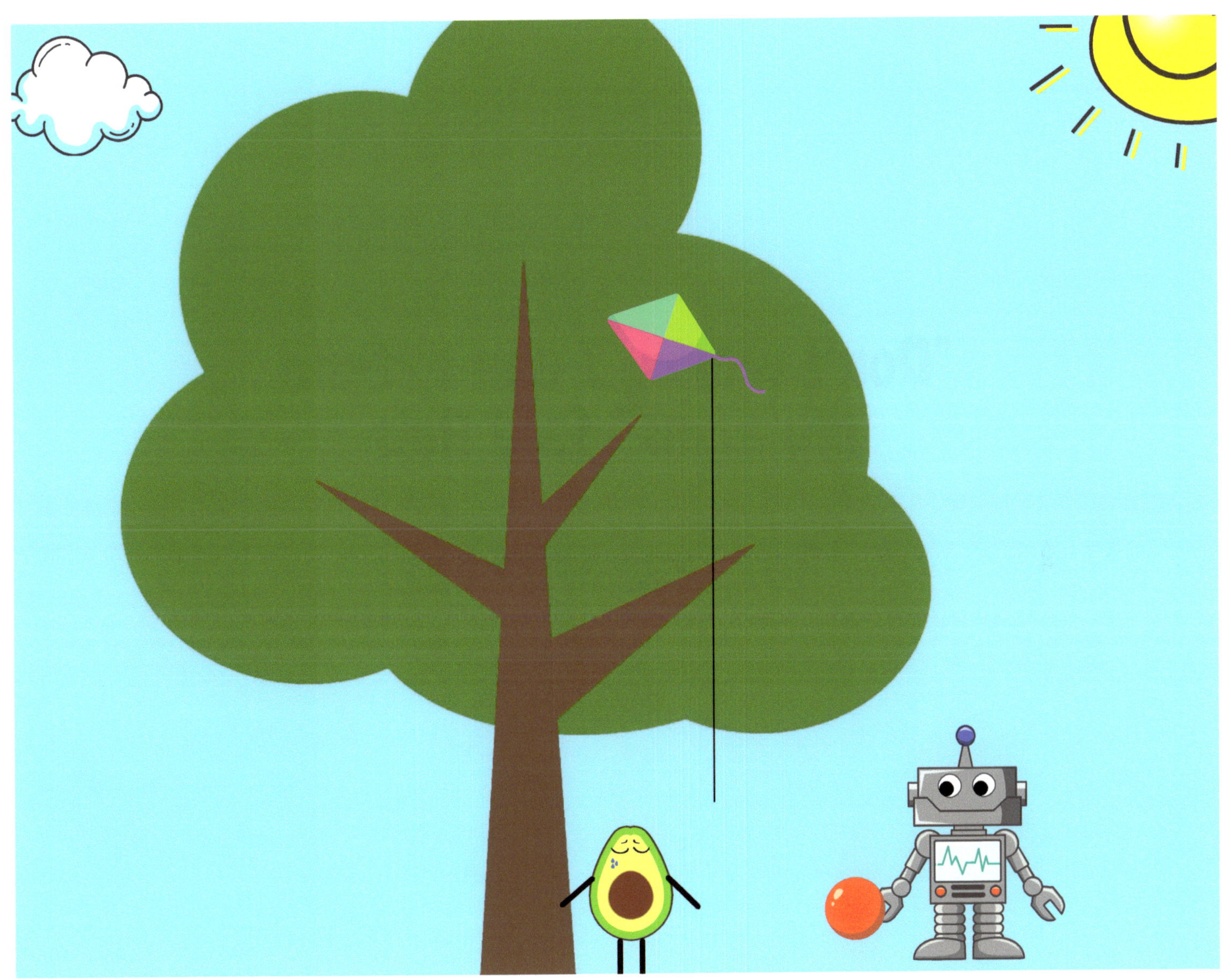

"Don't worry I can extend my arms." Said Rob

Buzzzzzzzzzzzz

"Here you go little buddy. What's your name?" Asked Rob

"My name is Allen, Thank you so much!" said Allen

"Let's be friends and play ball together." Said Rob

The End

www.ingramcontent.com/pod-product-compliance
Ingram Content Group UK Ltd.
Pitfield, Milton Keynes, MK11 3LW, UK
UKHW060102300726
14090UKWH00003B/352

* 9 7 9 8 5 3 5 1 3 5 7 7 9 *